Story by SHANA COREY

Pictures by MARK TEAGUE

SCHOLASTIC PRESS • NEW YORK

Published by Scholastic Press, a division of Scholastic Inc., *Publishers since 1920*. SCHOLASTIC and SCHOLASTIC PRESS and associated logos are trademarks and/or registered trademarks of Scholastic Inc.



Library of Congress Catalog Card Number: 00-058825

ISBN 0-439-26220-8

10 9 8 7 6 5 4 3 2 1 01 02 03 04 05

Printed in Mexico 49
First edition, August 2001
The text type was set in 18-point Martin Gothic Medium.
Book design by Kristina Albertson

For tracy mack,

one of the brightest stars in the universe

—SC

To Miss Garrells,

my first-grade teacher

—MT

It was a quiet day on Mars.
A dust storm swirled
across the ground.
A volcano blew purple gas
in the distance.
Suddenly, a flying cup
streaked across the sky.

It spun to a stop

and landed in a canyon.

*Creak!*

Its hatch opened.

Something, or some*one*, climbed out.

It was Horus.

"Are you sure you don't want me
to walk in with you?" asked Horus's mom.
"Mom!" said Horus.
"I am a first grader. I am not a baby!"
"Okay," said Horus's mom.
She stretched out her lips
and kissed Horus good-bye.
(She left a red suction mark.)

Horus rubbed the mark
off his forehead.
Then he headed into
Mariner Valley Elementary School.
He followed the twisty
canyon paths until
he found Pod 1.

Nergal, a friend from martiangarten,
was already inside.
Nergal waved his tentacles.
Horus waved his back.

A teacher floated over.

She had eyes in the back of her head.

And in the front.

And on the sides.

"Meep! Meep!" she said.

"I am your teacher, Ms. Vortex."

"Oip! Oip!" answered Horus. "I am Horus."
Ms. Vortex gave Horus a name tag.
Then she showed him
his thinking capsule.

Horus couldn't wait to get started.
"Where is the slime table?" he asked.
"Where are the snooze mats?
Where are the snacks?"
A girl Horus didn't know giggled.
Her name tag said "Tera."

"This isn't martiangarten anymore," she said.

"First graders are too big for those things."

Horus's tentacles drooped.

No slime table?

No snooze mats?

No snacks?

Before Horus could say anything,
Ms. Vortex clapped
her tentacles together.
"Okay, martians," she said.
"Let's get to work!"
Horus couldn't believe it.
In martiangarten,
there was no work until at least
the third day.

The rest of the day
didn't get any better.
In reading, Horus
was in the Beta group.
Tera and Nergal were both
in the Alpha group.
"Alphas are much brighter," said Tera.

In art, Horus drew a self-portrait.
"It doesn't look like you," said Tera.
"Maybe you should make it
a little lumpier."

There was no morning snack,
so by lunchtime
Horus was starving.
He was in such a hurry to eat
that he slurped his soup
up the wrong tentacle.
"Groboss!" said Tera.
Everyone except Nergal laughed.
Horus felt horrible.

After lunch, Horus was very tired.
But there was no snooze time
in first grade.
"Let's work on our numbers," said Ms. Vortex.
"4 + 2!" she called out. "5 + 3!"
Everyone rushed to form
the right answers.

Horus was so sleepy
that he accidentally
got stuck on 8.

After numbers, everyone
ran outside for recess.
On the way, Horus peeked inside
the martiangarten room.
The martiangartners
were hopping around
making animal sounds.
“Glump! Glump!” they said.
“Meelo! Meelo!”
Those were the days,
thought Horus sadly.

Horus's mom picked him up
after school.
"How was it?" she asked.
"Horrible," said Horus. "I'm not going back."
He refused to talk about it
for the rest of the night.

The next morning,
Horus's parents came into his room.
"Horus," said Horus's dad.
"I think you should give first grade
another try."
"I don't think so," said Horus.

"Horus," said Horus's mom.
"You can't live your life
with only a martiangarten education."
Horus thought about it.
He imagined eating snacks all day.
He imagined snoozing when he was tired.
He imagined getting a job
testing slime tables.
"Yebes, I can," he said.

"Horus, you have to go to school," said his mom.
"Nobo!" said Horus. "You can't make me!"
(Unfortunately, though, as it turned out,
she could.)

"Don't leave me here!" begged Horus
when they got to school.
Just then, another flying cup
pulled up beside them.
A giant blue martian dragged her
giant blue daughter out of the hatch.
"Pelly!" said the mother. "Behave!"
"Nobo!" screamed Pelly.
Horus stopped howling
and started watching.

Pelly's mom looked embarrassed.
"We just moved here from
the moon Phobos," she said.
"And Pelly is a little nervous
about starting first grade."
"I am not nervous!" wailed Pelly.
"Nobo one understands!"
Big blue teardrops
dripped out of her nose.

“I understand,” said Horus.

Pelly sniffled.

“You do?” she asked.

“Yebes,” said Horus.

“First grade will be terrible,” said Pelly.

“I know,” agreed Horus.

“It will be scary,” said Pelly.

“Tell me about it,” said Horus.

"The teacher will be mean," said Pelly.
Horus started to nod.
Then he remembered that Ms. Vortex
saved his life twice yesterday.
"Actually, the teacher is okay," he said.
Pelly looked doubtful.

“The work will be hard,” said Pelly.

Horus thought about getting stuck on 8.

Then he remembered

that he still got the answer right.

“It’s not that hard,” he admitted.

“I could get lost in the halls,” said Pelly.

“I could show you around,” offered Horus.

“Really?” said Pelly.

“Really,” said Horus.

Pelly's and Horus's moms smiled.
They offered to walk
Pelly and Horus inside.

“NOBO!” said Pelly and Horus
at the same time.
“We are not babies,” Pelly said.
“I’ve done this before,” added Horus.

So Horus and Pelly bounced
into Pod 1 together.
And from then on,
first grade started to look up.